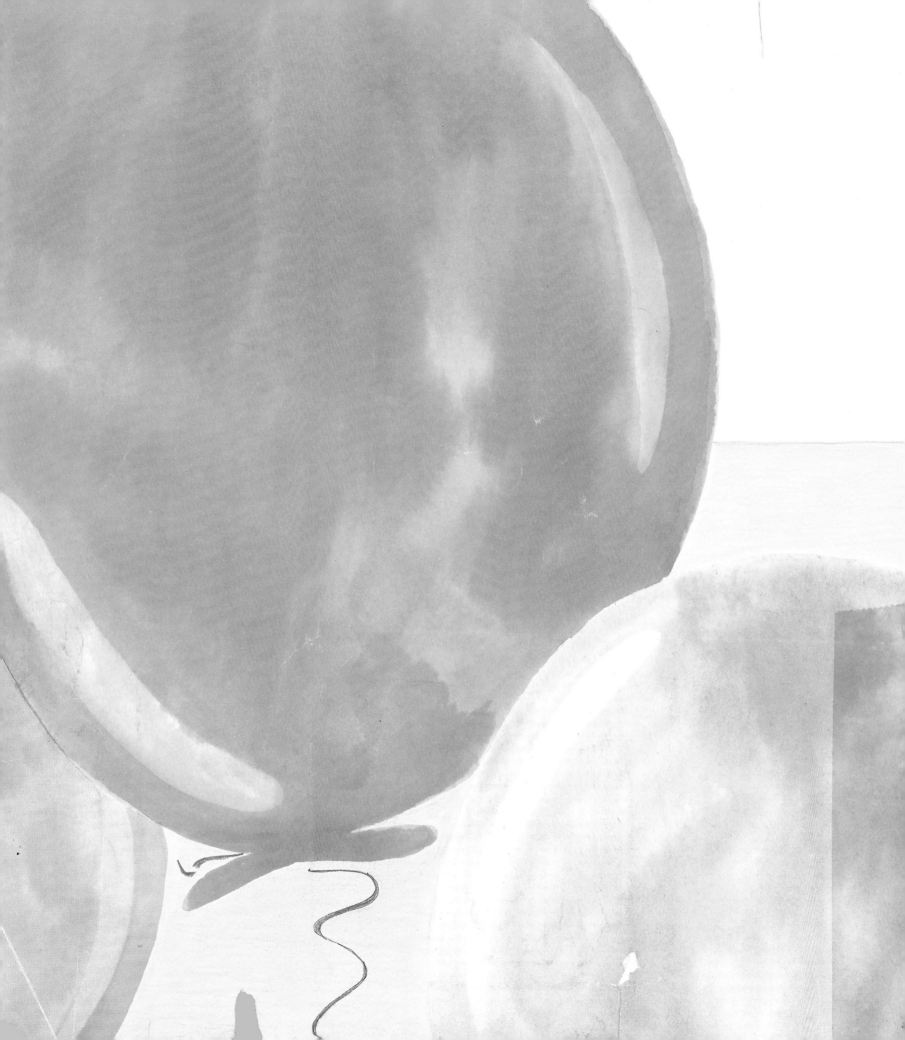

THE
BARN
PARTY

NANCY TAFURI

GREENWILLOW BOOKS · NEW YORK

WEE FOLKS

PETTING FARM

FOR CRISTINA

Colored pencils, watercolors, and a black pen were used
for the full-color art. The text type is Garamond Book.
Copyright © 1995 by Nancy Tafuri

Greenwillow Books, a division of William Morrow & Company, Inc.,
1350 Avenue of the Americas, New York, NY 10019.
Printed in Singapore by Tien Wah Press
First Edition 10 9 8 7 6 5 4 3 2 1

Library of Congress Cataloging-in-Publication Data
Tafuri, Nancy.
The barn party / by Nancy Tafuri.
p. cm.
Summary: Cristina's birthday is celebrated with
a party in the barn attended by all the animals.
ISBN 0-688-04616-9 (trade). ISBN 0-688-04617-7 (lib. bdg.)
[1. Birthdays—Fiction. 2. Domestic animals—Fiction.
3. Parties—Fiction.] I. Title.
PZ7.T117Bar 1995 [E]—dc20
94-25356 CIP AC

The barn
was decorated.
The birthday girl
was dressed.
The animals
were waiting.
It was time
for the party.

The guests arrived.

They hugged the lamb.
They petted the rabbits.
They played with the kittens
and fed the goat.

They played games
with the clown

and danced to the music.

Then everyone sat down,
and the cake was brought in.
They sang
HAPPY BIRTHDAY TO YOU,
HAPPY BIRTHDAY TO YOU,
HAPPY BIRTHDAY,
DEAR CRISTINA,
HAPPY BIRTHDAY TO YOU.

Cristina made a wish
and blew out the candles.
Everyone was eating
ice cream and cake—

when a balloon popped.
The lamb jumped.
The rooster crowed.

The ducks quacked.
The chicks scattered.
The rabbits hopped,

and everyone ran to catch them.

But where was the goat?

Not in the barn.

Not in the field. Not in the garden.

He was under
the apple tree,
opening
the presents!

And Cristina ran to help him.